Kamik's First Sled

Published by Inhabit Media Inc. • www.inhabitmedia.com

Inhabit Media Inc. (Iqaluit), P.O. Box 11125, Iqaluit, Nunavut, X0A 1H0
(Toronto), 146A Orchard View Blvd., Toronto, Ontario, M4R 1C3

Editors: Neil Christopher and Kelly Ward
Art director: Danny Christopher

We acknowledge the financial support of the Government of Canada through the Department of Canadian Heritage Canada Book Fund.

We acknowledge the support of the Canada Council for the Arts for our publishing program.

ISBN: 978-1-77227-020-4

Printed in Canada

Library and Archives Canada Cataloguing in Publication

Suluaryok, Matilda, author
Kamik's first sled / adapted from the memories of Matilda Suluaryok
; illustrated by Qin Leng.

ISBN 978-1-77227-020-4 (paperback)

1. Sled dogs--Juvenile fiction. 2. Sled dogs--Training--Juvenile fiction.
I. Leng, Qin, illustrator II. Title. III. Title: First sled.

PS8637.U5685K34 2015 jC813'.6 C2015-902480-3

Canada

Canada Council for the Arts
Conseil des Arts du Canada

Adapted from the memories of Matilda Sulurayok · Illustrated by Qin Leng

The sun bouncing off the bright white snow made Jake squint as he looked out over the first snowfall of autumn.

He had awoken that morning to see the tundra covered in a thick, soft blanket of white. It was the first real snowfall since Jake had started training his puppy, Kamik, and he was eager to see if Kamik could finally pull a sled.

Kamik leapt and spun in the new-fallen snow. He buried his nose in it and tossed it up over his head. Jake followed Kamik, trying to get him to settle down.

Kamik wriggled on his back for a moment and then bounced across the snow toward where Jake's uncle's dogs were tied.

"Hey! Wait a second!" Jake called. As he lunged to catch his scampering puppy, he landed on the snow with a thud.

As Jake lay face down in the snow, he heard someone coming down the steps of the house behind him. He got to his feet quickly, hoping that one of his cousins hadn't seen him fall.

"Jake, where did your puppy go?"

Jake was relieved to hear the loving voice of his grandmother, instead of a taunting cousin.

"He ran off, Anaanatsiaq. I wanted to see if I could teach him to pull your old qamutiik, but he won't sit still!"

"He's just doing what puppies do," Anaanatsiaq said, as she walked over to the group of dogs. Kamik was bouncing around the group, bowing and nipping at the other young dogs.

"See how he's not bothering the lead dog? He knows his place. He may be getting bigger, but he's still just a puppy, and puppies just want to play. When I was young, I helped my father train his young dogs by playing with them."

"But how can playing with a dog teach it anything? All Kamik ever does is play!"

"When our dogs were first born, we would bring them into the iglu and play with them. Then, when they were bigger, but still too small to pull a sled with a team, my brothers and I would have them pull us on sealskin toboggans. We called to them using our father's commands, 'harah, harah,' to make them go fast, 'hai' to turn left and 'avai' to turn right, and most importantly, 'whoa' to make them stop.

"We were all having fun, but the dogs were learning along the way! In the winter our parents would ask us to take them to the sea ice and have them dig in the snow to find seal breathing holes. They learned to listen to us, and then, when they were old enough, they were ready to listen to our father."

Jake called to Kamik using his Inuktitut name. "Tuhaaji, come," he said, in as stern a voice as he could muster. That was one command that Kamik definitely knew. As soon as Jake used Kamik's Inuktitut name, Kamik knew that Jake was serious. The puppy scampered over to Jake and sat at his feet, staring up into Jake's face.

"See, he's already learning," Anaanatsiaq beamed. "Why don't you take him out of town, away from the distraction of the other dogs, and see what else he can learn?"

Jake hadn't noticed the little package that his grandmother was carrying until she bent down and lashed it to Kamik's back like a backpack.

"One thing even a young dog can do is help carry a picnic. Be sure to watch him, though, because sled dogs can always hear and smell animals before we humans can, so he may run off after some game if you're not careful."

Jake waved goodbye to his grandmother as he walked down the road and out of town. Kamik ran ahead, sniffing at the ground as he went. They walked until Jake's grandmother's house was just a little square in the distance. Jake didn't think he should go so far that he couldn't see his way home, so he decided to stop for something to eat.

Jake called Kamik over and removed the pack that was lashed to Kamik's back. Inside, along with a piece of bannock for him and a small parcel of seal meat for Kamik, Jake found a piece of sealskin wrapped around an old sealskin sled-dog harness with a trace attached.

Anaanatsiaq had pinned a note to the hide. "Your first sled," it read.

Jake was so excited to try out the harness that he pulled Kamik's nose up from his seal meat to fit the harness over his head. It fit perfectly, and although he knew it was one of the old harnesses that his uncles no longer used, Jake thought it looked strong, and perfect for his first sled.

He quickly ate his bannock and made sure that Kamik didn't fill up too much on his meat. He didn't want Kamik getting too full and feeling lazy. They were going to need the energy for a long afternoon of mushing!

As soon as they were done eating, Jake tossed the pack over his shoulder and sat down on the sealskin with the trace in his hand. Anaanatsiaq had looped a rope through the sealskin, which he tied around his waist to keep the sled underneath him. Kamik, who seemed to be tried from the walk from town, stood looking at Jake happily, his tail wagging behind him.

"Harah!" Jake yelled.

Kamik simply stared and tilted his head a bit to the side.

"Harah!" Jake yelled again.

Still, Kamik did not move.

So Jake moved his sled so that he was sitting directly behind Kamik and there was no way for Kamik to turn and look at him. He curled the sealskin over his boots, pulled the trace so that it ran tightly across Kamik's back, took a deep breath, and yelled.

"Har—" before Jake could even finish his command, Kamik took off running as fast as he could!

The snow flew around Kamik's feet as they pounded across the tundra. Jake's cheeks felt the bite of the cold air as it whipped by him at an incredible speed. Kamik was doing it; he was pulling his first sled!

Jake yelled for Kamik to run faster, and he did. He tried controlling Kamik with the trace, guiding him to turn left or right while calling out "Hai!" or "Avai!"

After a few tries, Jake was sure that Kamik understood where he wanted him to go.

Jake ran Kamik in circles, tracing figure eights across the tundra. When Kamik got tired, they would rest for a while, and Kamik would eat a few mouthfuls of snow. Then, when he was ready to run again, Kamik would stand up and pull on the trace.

They were having so much fun that Jake didn't notice the dark grey clouds gathering overhead until the sky was nearly completely dark.

"Okay, boy, this will be the last run. We'd better get back into town soon," Jake said, staring up at the clouds.

Kamik stood up as he usually did, looking ready to pull. Then suddenly, something caught his attention. He turned his head quickly to the left, away from the direction of town, and sniffed the air. Before Jake could correct him, Kamik bolted in the direction of the scent, pulling Jake and the sled behind him.

"Whoa! Whoa!"

Jake yelled for Kamik to stop, but he suddenly realized that he had not taught him that command. All afternoon he had just let Kamik stop when he wanted to, and now Jake had no way of stopping him!

Jake yelled for Kamik to turn, hoping to steer him back to town, but Kamik did not seem to notice.

Jake thought about what his grandmother had said about Kamik running off after game if Jake wasn't careful. All Jake could do was hope that Kamik found the game quickly so that they didn't get too far away from town.

Suddenly Kamik stopped running and began digging in the snow. Jake dug his heels into the snow to stop the sled, jumped off, and looked where Kamik was digging.

"Tuhaaji!" Jake boomed as loudly as he possibly could. With that, Kamik stopped digging and edged back from the hole. Jake looked down into the hole just in time to see the back paws of an Arctic hare slipping deeper into its burrow.

"Great, a hare," Jake said. "We're not hunting today, Kamik." Jake was angry, and worried about the growing storm, but he was also a little bit proud of Kamik for finding game on his first try.

Jake knew he needed to get back to town as soon as possible, so he got back on the sled and yelled for Kamik to run as fast as he could.

"Harah, harah, harah!"

Jake and Kamik sped across the tundra in the direction of town. Kamik had followed the hare for so long that Jake could only just make out his grandmother's house in the distance.

As they travelled, the snow began to fall. At first it fell gently, but then it picked up, and soon the tundra, the sky, everything around Jake was pure white. Jake could only see a few feet in front of him, barely past Kamik's nose!

Jake called for Kamik to run faster. He remembered that his grandfather had told him that his dogs knew the way back to camp, even when he didn't know it, or couldn't guide them due to a storm. But Kamik was so young, and the tracks they had left on their way out of town had been blown away.

Jake was scared. All he could do was hold onto the trace and call for Kamik to run faster.

Suddenly, through the falling snow, Jake saw a building directly ahead of them. Kamik was running straight for it!

"Whoa!" Jake yelled, as he dug his heels into the snow. Jake slipped out of the rope that held the sealskin sled beneath him and left the sled on the ground. He ran toward the front of the house with Kamik. He hoped whoever lived here would give them shelter until the storm passed.

Through the whiteout, Jake could barely make out the railing of the porch. He ran up the stairs and grabbed the doorknob.

It wasn't until he and Kamik were on the porch that Jake recognized the smell of his grandmother's bannock. Kamik hadn't just brought them back to town, he had brought them right to Anaanatsiaq's house!

Anaanatsiaq opened the door and Jake ran to her for a hug.

"Anaanatsiaq! It started snowing, and I didn't know if we were going in the right direction! I couldn't see anything, and there were no tracks for Kamik to follow!"

"You have learned something that all mushers know well, Jake. Even when there are no tracks in the snow to follow, sled dogs are able to follow their trail back home with their sense of smell. I am so glad that Kamik got you home safely."

Anaanatsiaq bent down to give Kamik a thankful pat on the head.

As Jake went into the house to get warm and change out of his wet clothes, he decided to leave Kamik in the mud room, just inside the door to the house. He removed Kamik's harness, and gave him a small blanket to sleep on.

Kamik was soon going to be a strong, smart, sled dog, living with the rest of the dogs outside on the land. He was no longer a puppy who needed to be brought into the house.

"We'll play again tomorrow," Jake whispered, as Kamik settled down into his bed for the night. "Soon you'll be pulling more than just me and a sealskin. But that's not bad for your very first sled."

Contributors

Matilda Sulurayok is an elder who resides in Arviat, Nunavut. She was born and raised on the land near Chesterfield Inlet, Nunavut. She was raised by her parents and her grandmother, and she remembers much of what her grandmother taught her. Matilda's family lived a traditional life and raised several sled dogs. *Kamik's First Sled* is the first book to be based on Matilda's memories of traditional dog rearing. Matilda worked at the Andy Aulatjut Elder Centre as a caregiver for many years before she retired. She is a talented seamstress and enjoys sewing. She loves working with sealskins and makes beautiful kamiks.

Qin Leng was born in Shanghai and lived in France and Montreal. She now lives and works as a designer and illustrator in Toronto. Her father, an artist himself, was a great influence on her. She grew up surrounded by paintings, and it became second nature for her to express herself through art. She graduated from the Mel Hoppenheim School of Cinema and has received many awards for her animated short films and artwork. Qin has always loved to illustrate the innocence of children and has developed a passion for children's books. She has illustrated numerous picture books for publishers in Canada, the United States, and South Korea.

INHABIT
MEDIA